Cinder-Elephant

Samantha Newman

This edition published in 2021 by Arcturus Publishing Limited
26/27 Bickels Yard, 151–153 Bermondsey Street,
London SE1 3HA

Author: Samantha Newman
Illustrator: James Hearne
Cover illustrator: Chris Jevons
Designer: Jeni Child
Editor: Joe Harris

ISBN: 978-1-78950-244-2
CH006827NT
Supplier 13, Date 0421, Print run 10257

Printed in China

There once was a girl called Cinderella. She lived with her father in a beautiful house in a faraway kingdom.

Cinderella was a happy and boisterous girl, who loved nothing more than making people laugh. She danced silly dances and sang funny songs. Her singing sounded like a cat being given a bath, and her dances often ended in her smashing something, but her father didn't mind.

He laughed and sang along, and slapped his thigh. "You fill this house with laughter," he said, "And what could matter more than that?"

Cinderella had lived alone with her father ever since she was a tiny baby. But when he declared that he had fallen in love and would be marrying, she was delighted. And she was pleased to be gaining two stepsisters, Gertrude and Agatha.

On the day of the wedding, Gertrude and Agatha turned up in unusual outfits. Gertrude's dress had huge shoulder-pads like a bat's wings, and Agatha was wearing a stuffed pufferfish on her head.

"It's the latest courtly fashion," said Gertrude. "You wouldn't understand."

Cinderella was determined to show her new family how happy she was to have them. She sang a funny song at the reception, and danced enthusiastically. Everyone joined in, except for her new stepmother and sisters. As she led a conga around the room, Cinderella tripped and knocked over a whole table of cakes, covering Gertrude and Agatha in food.

Her father smiled sheepishly. “She made everyone happy,” he said, “and what could matter more than that?”

His new wife looked furious.

Not long after the wedding, Cinderella's father passed away. She was very upset, but had no time to cry because her new family immediately put her to work.

Her stepmother and stepsisters couldn't do anything around the house, they said, because it would spoil their fashionable clothes and scuff their pretty nails. They spent their time pouting into mirrors, painting self-portraits, and arguing about who had the most followers at court.

Cinderella was made to work hard from dawn until dusk, following their impossible orders.

"Cinderella, sweep the floor!" Gertrude cried.

"Cinderella,

dust the ceiling! NOW!" shouted Agatha.

"But Gertrude asked me to sweep the floor," Cinderella explained.

"Don't be so lazy, girl. Do them at the same time," snapped her stepmother.

Day in and day out, Cinderella was asked to do the impossible. She tried to carry on singing and dancing, remembering how her father used to enjoy it. But now there was no laughter in the house.

One day, Cinderella was serving up dinner. Gertrude had demanded fish pie, but Agatha had insisted that it *must not* smell like fish. Now, both of them were equally angry. Just then, a fancy-looking letter arrived.

Cinderella's stepmother read it out. "The King and Queen hereby invite every maiden in the kingdom to a ball at the royal palace tomorrow night! The time has come for Prince Charming to find a wife."

"A royal ball! I can't wait," cried Cinderella, almost dropping the fish pie in her excitement.

"You? At a ball?" said Gertrude, sneering.

Agatha snorted. "What's the point in you going? The Prince would never choose you as a wife."

“Yes, you’re so clumsy, you’d probably break his nose,” laughed Gertrude.

Cinderella felt hurt. “But every maiden is invited. That includes me.”

“It’s out of the question,” snapped her stepmother. “I won’t have you embarrassing us with your awful singing and dancing. My girls will go and the prince will choose one of them, I’m sure.”

Cinderella felt crushed.

It was the night of the ball. “Cinderella!” yelled Agatha. “This dress won’t do. I need something … dark, but in a bright way. Shocking, but in a subtle way. New, but old-fashioned.”

“Wherever will I find that?” Cinderella protested.

“Cinderella!” Gertrude stamped her foot. “I asked you to curl my hair right away!”

“But you’re rehearsing your ballroom

dancing," Cinderella pointed out, as her stepsister whirled past her.

"Yes, and I want you to curl my hair at the same time," snapped Gertrude. "There's no time to waste."

Cinderella sighed and heated up the curling iron. She tried to follow Gertrude round the room, but everyone just ended up singed—even the cat!

Cinderella's stepsisters yelled at her, but they were soon laughing again with the excitement of going to the ball. They piled into the carriage, taunting Cinderella that she wasn't coming, and raced away into the night.

Exhausted and upset, Cinderella ran outside and started to cry.

Cinderella's tears splashed onto the grass.

There was a tinkling sound and a winged lady appeared, holding a wand.

"Who are you?" said Cinderella, in astonishment.

"Sorry, deary, I didn't catch that," said the lady. "My ears are just *full* of fairy dust today. That's right, I'm a fairy! Your Fairy Godmother, in fact. And I'm here to help you go to the ball!"

Cinderella gave a sad smile. "That's very kind, Fairy Godmother. But it's a long way and I have no coach to take me to the palace."

The Fairy Godmother flitted about excitedly. "Let's fix that right now!"

She waved her wand at a large pumpkin in the vegetable patch. There was another tinkling sound and the pumpkin transformed into a giant BUG!

Cinderella gasped, but her Fairy Godmother was smiling encouragingly.

"You wanted a roach to take you to the palace, didn't you, deary?"

She didn't have the heart to correct her Fairy Godmother. "Thank you," she said, "but I can't use this, um, roach ... because I don't have a driver."

The Fairy Godmother pointed her wand at a rat scurrying through the vegetable patch.

Sparks flew and the rat transformed into … a man wearing a wetsuit, snorkel, and flippers.

"One diver!" announced the Fairy Godmother, proudly. "Now, what else will you need, to fit in at the ball?"

Before Cinderella could open her mouth, the diver said, "A noble lady would have smartly dressed servants."

The Fairy Godmother waved her wand at two worms. With a tinkle of magic, they turned into snakes, wearing shirts and ties!

"Two smartly dressed serpents!" she beamed. "What else?"

Cinderella and the diver exchanged a look. Cinderella could tell that he didn't want to correct the good-hearted fairy either.

"Um, what about some magnificent ponies?" she suggested, hesitantly.

There was another tinkle of magic, and in Cinderella's arms appeared... an enormous bowl of *macaroni and cheese*.

"What an entrance you'll make!" cried the Fairy Godmother.

The Fairy Godmother turned to Cinderella. "Now, would you like a different outfit? I don't know what's in fashion these days."

Cinderella opened her mouth, but the diver got there first again.

"She should arrive in a gown, wearing nice slippers."

The Fairy Godmother waved her wand.

"Upside down!" she cried, "Wearing glass flippers!"

With a whoosh, Cinderella found herself head over heels! And on her feet, instead of slippers, a pair of glass flippers twinkled.

Cinderella really didn't want to be ungrateful but being upside down was very uncomfortable. The diver took a breath. "Not another word, you!" she cried. "I'm tired of being funny, I need to look *elegant*!"

"Oh, why didn't you say so?" asked the Fairy Godmother. She waved her wand again.

Cinderella was flipped the right way up. She looked down. This time, she was wearing a beautiful dress, but something was wrong ...

Her feet were oddly thick and stubby. Her arms were, too, and her nose felt very large and ... long? She peered into the pond and gasped with horror. Looking back at her was ... an elephant!

The Fairy Godmother flapped her hands. "Now you must hurry! The magic will only last until the final stroke of midnight, so you must be home by then."

She waved her wand and Cinder-Elephant was whisked up through the air and set down on the roach's back, the bowl of macaroni in her arms.

The diver climbed up in front of her. The two smart serpents slithered up behind.

This was not the way Cinder-Elephant had imagined going to the ball, but she couldn't bear to upset her Fairy Godmother, so she said, "Thank you so much."

"Anything for my dearest god-daughter. Now, go and have fun." She

disappeared in a sparkle of silver.

“We’re off!” whooped the diver, as the roach scuttled forward along the road.

Cinder-Elephant was determined to enjoy herself. Elephant or not, this might be the only time she would ever be invited to a royal ball!

The palace looked truly beautiful, but everyone inside looked very serious. The white marble columns were wreathed in white flowers, and a very stern-looking band were playing a slow, sensible tune.

All the guests had formed a line to meet the royal family. Prince Charming was dressed in a fine purple tunic, and looked very handsome.

Cinder-Elephant gazed all around her as she stepped through the doorway. "Wow," she said, louder than she meant to.

Dozens of faces turned in her direction. Whispers came floating through the air.

"What's an *elephant* doing here?"

"Look at it!"

Cinder-Elephant saw her stepsisters looking aghast.

She felt hot and embarrassed. She'd really hoped to have a nice time at the ball.

She decided to leave right away, but then she saw Prince Charming looking at her. Did he look ... lonely?

It would be rude to leave now, Cinderella told herself, sternly. *I'll say hello and then go home.*

When Cinder-Elephant reached the front of the line, Prince Charming smiled at her and she felt her heart skip a beat. Unfortunately, so did her feet. She tripped and knocked the prince over, covering him in macaroni!

"I'm so sorry, Your Highness," Cinder-Elephant cried. She tried to help him up, but they both slipped again on the cheese sauce of the macaroni and fell on their bottoms.

To Cinder-Elephant's surprise, Prince Charming started laughing. She laughed too.

"This is fun!"

He spun in a circle. Cinder-Elephant did too. "It *is* fun!" she laughed.

"I never get to play like this," beamed Prince Charming. "Princes aren't supposed to."

"I see," said Cinder-Elephant, slyly picking up some macaroni. "So, I suppose they aren't meant to have food fights either?" She hurled the pasta at him.

Laughing again, he grabbed a handful of his own. All the people of the court couldn't help but start to laugh. Soon, everyone was in hysterics, watching the prince chasing the elephant around the room. Everyone, that is, except for Cinderella's stepsisters.

Once they had tired of throwing pasta at each other, Prince Charming helped Cinder-Elephant up and looked into her eyes. “Would you like to dance?”

Cinder-Elephant could barely believe her flappy ears. She’d expected the prince to be pleasant ... but she hadn’t thought he’d be this much fun!

"I don't really know how to dance," she admitted. "Only the silly dancing I do at home."

Prince Charming's eyes lit up. "Would you show me?"

Cinder-Elephant felt a little silly in the grand ballroom, but she did a funny wiggle and kicked her legs high. She threw in a twirl, then a jump, and before she knew it, she was bounding around the room.

"Brilliant!" cried Prince Charming, as he joined in.

They danced and danced until, through the music and laughter, Cinder-Elephant heard the clock striking midnight. Oh no! She'd completely forgotten about her curfew.

"I have to go!" she exclaimed, turning and running out of the ballroom.

"Wait!" Prince Charming called.

Cinder-Elephant couldn't bear to turn back as she raced down the palace steps. In her haste, one of the glass flippers slipped from her foot as she ran. She scrambled up onto the roach's back. "Go!" Cinder-Elephant cried.

As they raced away into the night, the magic started to undo itself. With a POP the smart serpents became worms again. A moment later, the diver was a rat and, just as they turned into the garden, the roach transformed back into a pumpkin.

Cinder-Elephant tumbled to the ground and when she sat up, she saw she was herself again, in her old dress. The only sign that the magic had ever been there was the single glass flipper, which she quickly hid.

Cinderella's stepsisters were full of talk about the strange happenings at the ball when they came home. They taunted Cinderella for missing it.

Cinderella smiled secretly to herself. Little did they know …

The next morning, word was sent from the palace that Prince Charming wanted to meet the wonderful elephant-maiden again.

Cinderella could hardly believe it! She wished she could run and tell the prince that it was her, but she wasn't allowed to leave the house.

Several days passed and when Prince Charming's dream maiden didn't come forward, he decided to visit every house in the kingdom to search for her, taking the glass flipper with him.

"The maiden who fits this flipper will be the one," he announced, confidently. "Surely no one else in the kingdom could possibly have feet *this* large."

When he and his men arrived at Cinderella's house, her stepsisters fought to try the flipper on first. Of course, it didn't fit either of them and they both sulked.

"I wonder if I might try it on?" said Cinderella, softly.

"Nonsense," snapped her stepmother.

"I would like every maiden to try the flipper," said Prince Charming, kindly. He held it out.

“I forbid you to try it on!” shrieked Cinderella’s stepmother, grabbing her by the arm and trying to drag her away.

“Stop!” said Cinderella, “I’ve had enough of being pushed around!”

The flipper slid onto Cinderella’s foot, which grew bigger. It was a perfect fit! The fairy’s magic flowed from the slipper into her body, and she was suddenly transformed

back into an elephant. And it felt *great*. Her stepmother let go of her arm, having realized that there was no way she'd be able to drag her anywhere.

One of the soldiers stepped forward. "Your Highness, your parents will never allow you to marry this galumphing creature!"

"You're not the only one who's tired of being told how to act," said Prince Charming.

He kissed Cinder-Elephant on her trunk. The magical glow surrounded both of them, and then he was transformed into an elephant, too!

"I'm not Prince Charming any more," he said, laughing. "Now, I'm Prince Charging!"

The two elephants stampeded out of the house, hand in hand.

A year later, Cinder-Elephant and Prince Charging got married. They asked the Fairy Godmother for confetti and bells at their wedding. Instead, they were showered with spaghetti and smells, but it was still the most perfect day ever.

Both elephants sang silly songs about their love for each other, danced together, and ate mountains of macaroni cheese. And all of their guests agreed it was the best wedding they had ever been to.